ATTACK OF THE 50-FOOT TEACHER

LISA PASSEN

HENRY HOLT AND COMPANY

Henry Holt and Company, LLC
Publishers since 1866
115 West 18th Street, New York, New York 10011
www.henryholt.com

Library of Congress Cataloging-in-Publication Data
Passen, Lisa. Attack of the 50-foot teacher / Lisa Passen.
Summary: On Halloween a spaceship turns Miss Irma Birmbaum,
the cruelest teacher in the world, into a 50-foot monster,
inspiring terror in her students. [1. Teachers—Fiction. 2. Schools—Fiction.
3. Halloween—Fiction. 4. Unidentified flying objects—Fiction.] I. Title.
PZ7.P26937At 2000 [E]—dc21 99-24467

ISBN 0-8050-6100-2 (hardcover)
3 5 7 9 10 8 6 4 2
ISBN 0-8050-7260-8 (paperback)
1 3 5 7 9 10 8 6 4 2
First published in hardcover in 2000 by Henry Holt and Company
First Owlet paperback edition—2003
Designed by Donna Mark
Printed in the United States of America on acid-free paper. ∞
The artist used watercolor on 300-pound hot-press Lanaquarelle paper
to create the illustrations for this book.

To Rubi

M iss Irma Birmbaum was
the toughest teacher in town.

"Sit in your seats, children. No talking!
Pass your homework assignments forward.
Open your books to page 24. Read!"

Miss Irma Birmbaum never smiled.

All the children were afraid of her.

But Miss Irma Birmbaum wasn't afraid of anyone or anything.

On the chalkboard:

October 31 - Homework
History - Read Chapter 13
Math - Questions 20 - 31
Sp___s

It was Halloween.

And it was a school day.

The children were eager for school to be over.

Everyone was excited about going trick-or-treating.

Just before the bell rang for the end of school, Miss Irma Birmbaum wrote the day's homework assignment on the chalkboard. "For tomorrow, read chapter 13 of your history books. Be prepared for a test. Answer questions 20 to 31 in your math workbooks. And learn the new words on your spelling sheet."

"Homework on Halloween!" moaned the children as they left the room. "Miss Irma Birmbaum is the cruelest teacher in the world."

Miss Irma Birmbaum stayed behind and checked science tests.

It was very late when she left.
The road home was blocked off.
Miss Irma Birmbaum took a detour.

The unfamiliar path was dark and deserted. In her rearview mirror, Miss Irma Birmbaum saw something odd hovering in the sky.

A bright, glowing spaceship quickly passed the car. It landed right in front of her.

"Move this vehicle and move it RIGHT NOW!" she shouted.

Miss Irma Birmbaum really wasn't afraid of anyone or anything.

The spaceship began to glow more brightly. It started spinning around at a fantastic speed and took off into the night.

Miss Irma Birmbaum stepped back.

She felt funny.

Her stockings started to itch.

She took off her glasses and rubbed her eyes.

Miss Irma Birmbaum put her glasses back on and looked down. Her car was the size of a toy. The trees were as small as azalea bushes. She had grown incredibly tall. Miss Irma Birmbaum was now a 50-foot teacher!

As Miss Irma Birmbaum walked toward town, the earth shook beneath her giant feet.

Rubi Flint was the first to see her.

Rubi dropped her bag of Halloween candy and ran to warn the others.

Cars screeched to a halt.
People looked out their windows and screamed.

"Miss Birmbaum is coming! Miss Birmbaum is coming!" shouted Rubi.

"Big deal," said Johnny O'Leary. "We still have enough time to finish our homework."

"You don't understand!" exclaimed Rubi. "Miss Birmbaum is a . . . Miss Birmbaum is a . . ."

"LOOK AT MISS BIRMBAUM!" screamed Sheryl Shackmeyer.

"Miss Birmbaum is a 50-FOOT TEACHER!"

"EEEKKKKKK!" screamed the children.

"I told you we should have done our homework!" declared Rubi.

Miss Irma Birmbaum staggered toward them.

"Johnny! Johnny O'Leary!" Miss Irma Birmbaum's voice echoed loudly through the dark sky.

She reached down and grabbed poor Johnny. "What are you doing out so late at night, Johnny?"

"I'm sorry, Miss Birmbaum! I'm gonna go home right now and finish my homework. I promise!"

Miss Irma Birmbaum turned toward the others. "And the rest of you! Do your parents know you're wandering about at this unearthly hour? I'm taking you all to the principal!"

She scooped up the other children and put them in her purse. Her enormous legs stepped over houses and trees until she reached Main Street.

Miss Irma Birmbaum rang the doorbell of Principal Renfield's home.

The principal opened his front door.

"Yes?" He looked up. Way up.

"Miss Birmbaum! What has become of you?"

The 50-foot teacher placed the children on Principal Renfield's front lawn. "These children are out alone at night! And they haven't done their homework."

"Good grief, woman!" exclaimed Principal Renfield. "Who gives homework on Halloween? Don't you remember what it was like to be a child? Don't you remember the fun of wearing your costume and trick-or-treating and eating so much candy your stomach got sick?"

Halloween? thought Miss Irma Birmbaum. It was Halloween?

Happy memories of her girlhood flashed through her mind. Costumes. Candy. Tricks and treats.

Had it been that long ago? How could she have forgotten?

The giant teacher stepped back.

She felt funny.

Her stockings started to itch again.

"Attention!" Miss Irma Birmbaum shouted.

Every child on every street stopped to listen.

"Your homework assignment for tonight is . . . to have as much fun as you can! After all, it's Halloween. And Halloween comes only once a year!"

"Is Miss Birmbaum feeling okay?" Johnny asked Principal Renfield. The principal smiled.

Miss Irma Birmbaum took a flashlight out of her purse. "You children go on trick-or-treating. I'll look after you to make sure you're safe."

The children couldn't believe their good fortune! And the parents were pleased that the trick-or-treaters wouldn't have to wander about in the dark. All agreed it was the best, best Halloween they ever had.

Just past midnight, Miss Irma Birmbaum fell asleep in front of the school.

When she awoke the next morning, she had shrunk to her normal size.

"What an extraordinary experience I've had!"

When the children came to class, they were disappointed to see the same old Miss Irma Birmbaum they had always known. The one who never smiled.

"Sit in your seats, children. No talking!"

Miss Irma Birmbaum walked to the front of the classroom. She bent down and scratched her leg.

"Did everyone have a happy Halloween?" she asked.

"YES!" shouted the children.

"So did I!" Miss Irma Birmbaum said. And she smiled.